This book belongs to:

_____

_____

Guvna B and Emma Borquaye

Illustrated by Aaron Cushley

Where Grandad Lives

Ezra and Zadie stepped out into the fresh air on a warm summer's day. 'Goodbye Grandad!' they shouted.

CLARKE Rd

Zadie smiled. She always liked visiting her Grandad —
especially when he gave her ice-cream.
'Ezra, where does your Grandad live?' she asked.

'Oh,' said Ezra, 'my Grandad lives somewhere really special.'
'I bet I can find out where!' said Zadie. 'I know, I have an idea! *Follow me!*'
Zadie zipped ahead and Ezra skipped behind.

'Does your Grandad live here?' asked Zadie as they stood in front of the tallest, swirliest treehouse that Ezra had ever seen.

'Wow, this is special! But, no,' Ezra laughed, 'he doesn't live here.'
They jumped and climbed all the way
to the top of the treehouse.

The children giggled as they took the long curly slide
down to the bottom. Then Zadie had another idea.
'OK, I think I know where your Grandad lives . . . *Follow me!*'

Zadie zipped ahead and Ezra skipped behind.

'Does your Grandad live here?'
'A sweet shop!' said Ezra. 'My Grandad
doesn't live here, but let's buy some treats!'
The special shop had sweets of all
different colours and patterns
in big jars that lined the walls.

Zadie thought for a long time. She tried to think about the most special place that she had EVER been to. Then she shouted, 'I've got it! I know where your Grandad lives! *Follow me!*'

Zadie zipped ahead and Ezra skipped behind.

'Does your Grandad live here?' asked Zadie
as they arrived at a big brown gate.

Zadie was sure that she had found
the MOST special place.

But before Ezra could even answer,
Zadie knocked on the gate.

Knock, knock, knock...

There was a deep rumbling sound.

DORRET

PJ :)

RGW×

G∪B

DAISY

G

MARY

LOST CAT

KENNIE

'An alpaca!' Ezra said in excitement as he reached up to stroke the furry neck. 'Even though this place is really special with amazing animals, my Grandad doesn't live here.'

Zadie and Ezra had walked a long way and their feet were getting tired.
Their tummies grumbled for food that wasn't sweets or ice-cream,
but they reached the top of a hill and looked for a place to rest.

'Ezra, I have thought of all the most special places that I know, but your Grandad isn't at ANY of them' sighed Zadie. 'I don't have any more ideas.
Tell me, where does your Grandad live?'

Ezra smiled. He wanted to tell Zadie all about his Grandad,
and now he was ready to answer.

Ezra placed his hands on his chest and said in a loud voice,
'my Grandad lives right here in my heart.'

For the first time all day, Zadie was speechless
and she listened closely as Ezra explained.

'A little while ago, my Grandad died. And I really miss him. But just before he left, he told me . . .

"Your heart's got a loving-place, a forever-space where your special people are with you now and always."'

Zadie's eyes widened and she leaned in to hear more.

'When you love someone,
even though you don't see
them anymore, the memories
are in your heart forever.'

'I think it's the most special place because even though I can't
see Grandad anymore, he's with me wherever I go.'

Zadie was quiet — and in a careful voice she asked Ezra,
'What does it feel like to have someone living in your heart?'

Ezra looked thoughtful. 'I miss him, and I would prefer it if Grandad still lived in his house. But he doesn't.'

'Sometimes when I remember Grandad in my heart I feel happy — and that's OK.'

'Sometimes it can make me feel really sad — and that's OK.'

'And then sometimes I don't feel anything
at all — and that's OK too.'

'Because I know that one day I will get to see Grandad again.

'It will be a place so amazing and
more wonderful than I can imagine.

There aren't enough colours to paint a picture
or words to describe it.

But until then . . .'

'My heart's got a loving-place, a forever-space where my special people are with me now and always.'

Zadie gave a big smile. Ezra stood up and said,
'My Grandad used to say that alpacas hum
when they're happy. Shall we go and see?!'

Zadie and Ezra zipped down the hill humming Grandad's favourite tune.

As we do life with our own son Ezra, we hope we can continue to have conversations with him about the loved ones we've lost. Though this can bring sadness, as well as happiness, we believe it's an important part of keeping their legacies alive and it can help children understand more about who they are and the special people who came before them. We hope that this book is a helpful tool as you navigate life, grief and raising little ones.

We have a firm hope that one day we will see our loved ones again, but in the meantime, cherishing those memories of Grandad helps to keep him 'living in our hearts'.

Guvna B and Emma Borquaye

THAT'S OK TOO . . .

Our hope with this book is to show children that it's OK to feel all sorts of emotions when they remember someone they love who isn't with them any longer. There is no right way to 'live with someone in your heart' and it shouldn't be something you're afraid to explore or share with others.

Even if your children are too young to have personal memories of a loved one, this book is still important for you as a parent. We know from our own experience of grief that there can be a fear of forgetting a loved one who was so significant in our lives, and we have a desire to keep their memory alive. So how do we navigate this with our children?

Children are naturally inquisitive, and they often want to know more about who they are and what came before them. When we share our fond memories and stories of those we love but see no longer, it helps our children to build their own picture of who that person was and why they were important. These kinds of conversations also serve as an encouragement to children — that everyone's life has an impact on the people around them and the world!

PEANUT BRITTLE AND DAISIES

You'll notice in the book that Ezra gathers small reminders of Grandad during the story. Physical memory prompts are a great way for children to work through their grief. You could consider creating a memory box or look together for shells, sticks or whatever is significant to you when you are in a place of shared memories.

GRANDAD IS NOT IN HIS HOUSE . . .

Younger children may seem to understand that the death of a loved one means they won't see them physically anymore, but at other times they can appear to forget and need a reminder. Don't shy away from talking frankly about the fact that things have changed but also try to explore how the relationship can continue as you remember your loved one together.

GRANDAD IS THERE ON EZRA'S TERMS

In this story, the memories and 'chats' with Grandad are all on Ezra's terms, initiated by him. Someone who 'lives in your heart' does not have any independent control and is not a voice or entity. This might be of concern to some children, and you might need to reassure them.

DO ALPACAS HUM?

At the end of their conversation, Ezra quickly moves from talking about something very deep and special to something completely different. This is a very normal coping mechanism for children; they guard themselves against being overwhelmed by grief through seeming to jump in and out of it.

First published in Great Britain in 2023 by Hodder & Stoughton
An Hachette UK company

1

A CIP catalogue record for this title is available from the British Library

Hardback ISBN 978 1 529 39513 6
eBook ISBN 978 1 529 39515 0

Printed and bound in China

Hodder & Stoughton policy is to use papers that are natural, renewable and recyclable products and made
from wood grown in sustainable forests. The logging and manufacturing processes are expected
to conform to the environmental regulations of the country of origin.

Hodder & Stoughton Ltd
Carmelite House
50 Victoria Embankment
London EC4Y 0DZ

www.hodderfaithyoungexplorers.co.uk